PRESENTED TO

....

FROM

....

Cover and interior design: Chris Gilbert - UDG | DesignWorks

Published in 2004 by Broadman & Holman Publishers,
Nashville, Tennessee

DEWEY:CE
SUBHD: EASTER \ JESUS CHRIST – RESURRECTION

All rights reserved. Printed in Perú

ISBN 0-8054-2680-9

1 2 3 4 5   08 07 06 05 04

THE
EASTERVILLE
MIRACLE

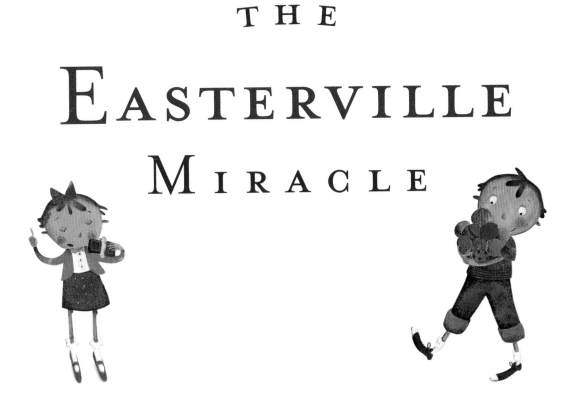

MELODY CARLSON

Illustrations by Susan Reagan

Broadman & Holman Publishers | Nashville, Tennessee

Once, a long, long time ago, and somewhere far away,

In a place that never was (or so some people say),

Tucked neatly in the shadows, beneath a tall green hill,

Sat a quaint and little town—its name was Easterville.

Now no one in this tiny town knew how it got its name,

But as long as they remembered it always was the same.

Yet one thing the people knew—their town sure did it right.

For when it came to Easter, *Easterville was quite the sight!*

Now Easterville grew merry in the early part of spring,

When flowers started budding and the birds began to sing.

And in the storefront windows, cheerful colors would appear,

And everyone felt full of joy as Easter Day grew near.

Eggs of pink and green and red, yellow, orange and blue,

Bunny rabbits stuffed with fluff—fuzzy and brand new,

Baskets decked out beautifully with bright and sparkling bows,

Chocolates in the shapes of chicks stood ready in neat rows.

All these sights in Easterville filled each child with glee

Little ones would stop and stare and giggle happily.

Time to buy some shiny shoes, a dress with lace upon it,

A brand new suit, a bright bow tie, a lovely Easter bonnet.

Much ado and lots of fuss and sometimes a few tears,

It was the way of Easterville, had been like this for years.

Still most people never asked just how it got that way,

But Easter morn in Easterville became a hectic day.

Then one day, a boy named Sam felt troubled and confused.

He didn't like this Easter fuss—he didn't feel amused.

"Oh, why, oh, why?" he asked his mom. "Why go to all this trouble?

All this goofy Easter stuff will soon just turn to rubble."

Sam's mom blinked, then shrugged and said, "I guess I just don't know.

This is what we've always done. It's just the way to go."

But Sam just frowned and shook his head. To him it made no sense.

All this fuss for bunnies and eggs—it felt like pure nonsense.

So then Sam marched all through the town, and asked each one he knew,

"What is the point of Easter? The cause for all we do?"

"It's for the eggs," said one boy. "Candy!" said the next.

"It's for the clothes," said a girl. "Easter Bunny!" yelled the rest.

But when Sam asked how it began, each person there agreed,

That not a single one recalled—no one had seen the need.

"This is crazy," cried poor Sam. "There has to be a reason

For the things we do each year to mark the Easter season."

The oldest woman in the town now paused and scratched her head.

"Sam makes a point and makes me think. I do recall," she said.

"Back when I was a little girl, it wasn't quite this way.

It seems that something has been lost about this holiday."

"I just knew it," said young Sam. "I knew that it was wrong.

I knew there must be something else more special all along!"

But all the other people laughed—they laughed with glee galore.

Not a single one believed that Easter could mean more.

"Don't listen to them, Sammy," said the woman in a hush.

"I know just who can help you—and by Easter, if you rush.

The old man's name is Henry. He lives up on the hill.

At least I think he used to—I'm not sure he's living still."

"Old Henry had a tiny house, and it was made of stone,

He lived upon the hilltop—he lived there all alone."

So, Sam began his journey. He gave the hike his all,

Climbing up the steep, green slope, prepared to make this call.

And when Sam reached the summit and saw the house of rock,

He went up to the wooden door, took a deep breath, and knocked.

"Hello there," said an ancient man who wore a kindly smile.

"Welcome to my humble home, no one's been here in awhile."

"Hello, dear sir, my name is Sam, and I have come to ask you

What is Easter all about? Someone told me that you knew."

The old man stroked his snowy beard and said, "It's quite a tale,

But others would not listen—although I know it well."

Then Henry told the story of when God sent His own Son

And how He lived among us and all the deeds He'd done.

"And after years of teaching some and healing many others,

He gave His life for everyone—His sisters and His brothers."

"Upon a cross, He took our sins. 'Forgive them, God,' He said.

He died—but three days later, He rose up from the dead!

So now when Easter season comes—the same time every spring,

It's Jesus we should celebrate. His praises we should sing!"

With wide eyes Sam just listened—he sat there in a daze—

And after hearing that great tale, he really was amazed.

"There's nothing wrong," old Henry said, "with bunnies, eggs, and things,

But something's wrong when we forget the One who's King of kings."

"What can we do?" demanded Sam. "To share this news with all?

I know that you are very old. I know that I am small—

But surely there is something—what is there we can do

To help the folks remember—to share this truth anew."

Old Henry looked around him and then he slowly stood.

"I think I have a thought, my son. An idea that is good."

He whispered in the boy's right ear, he told him of his plan.

He asked the boy to help him for he was an ancient man.

Both man and boy worked all night long on that Easter's Eve,

Sam didn't know how this would help the townsfolk to believe.

But still he never questioned, for he trusted the old man.

He followed every order as he helped him work his plan.

But shortly before sunrise, weary Sam fell to the ground.

He went to sleep, deep and hard, and barely made a sound.

And then when he awakened with the sun upon his face,

He looked around but saw no one—Henry had left this place!

Not only was the old man gone, his house was gone as well.

Had he truly been there? Poor Sam could hardly tell.

Were the house and man for real, or something he'd just dreamed?

Today, nothing made much sense—nothing was as it seemed.

Sam trudged down the green hillside, down to the town below.

He felt confused and lonely—he didn't even know

That this fine day was Easter—a day to celebrate.

He didn't know and didn't care if he was very late.

But when he reached the little town, he saw a quiet crowd,

All were looking up the hill, some whispering aloud.

"A miracle," said someone. "Where could that have come from?"

"And look at how it glistens just like diamonds in the sun!"

Sam turned and looked behind him, he looked up at the hill,

And what he saw took his breath—it made his heart stand still.

A giant cross of shimmering stones—so beautiful, so grand!

Now Sam fully understood the plan that Henry planned.

And while Sam had the people there, all gathered in one place,

He told the truth about God's Son—about His love and grace.

And since that day, so long ago, all those in Easterville

Love to hear the story of the cross upon the hill!

For God so loved the world

that he gave his one and only Son,

that whoever believes in him

shall not perish but

have eternal life.

JOHN 3:16 (NIV)